# An Enchanted Hair Tale

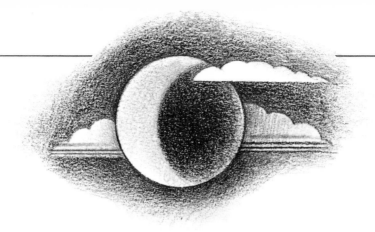

# An Enchanted Hair Tale

By Alexis De Veaux

Pictures by Cheryl Hanna

Harper & Row, Publishers     New York

An Enchanted Hair Tale

Library of Congress Cataloging-in-Publication Data
De Veaux, Alexis, 1948–
    An enchanted hair tale.

    Summary: Sudan suffers when people ridicule his
strange-looking hair, but he comes to accept and
enjoy its enchantment.
    [1. Hair—Fiction.    2. Self-acceptance—Fiction]
I. Hanna, Cheryl, ill.    II. Title.
PZ7.D497En  1987        [E]        85-45824
ISBN 0-06-021623-9
ISBN 0-06-021624-7 (lib. bdg.)

2  3  4  5  6  7  8  9  10

To Irene
   Ryan
   Fatima
   T J
   Ayodele
   and Egypt
      A D V

For
   Brandon
   and Jennifer
      C H

# An Enchanted Hair Tale

Once in time lived a boy named Sudan,
who had his father's eyes
and had his father's lips
and had hair,
a wild mysterious,
like his mother.

What a fabric was Sudan's hair,
what a fan daggle
of locks and lions and lagoons.

So enchanted
so very
very it was
so enchanted
so very
very.

It giggled when he talked
and roared when he walked
and often sprouted
wings.

B
ut grown-ups were afraid of it
and didn't like it
and whispered,
"How ugly. How unsightly. It's uncombed."

So the neighbors frowned
and the children teased,
and wherever Sudan went,
people saw his head;
they pointed and said,
"He's strange. He's queer. He's different."

Naturally all this talk
made him blue
and mad
and just plain evil,
so he cried a lot
and he fought a lot, too.

And one day
when the grown-ups made him
mummy mad
and the children made him
elephant evil,
he growled and grunted and stomped
and said,
"LEAVE ME ALONE! STOP MESSIN' WITH MY HEAD!"

And though his mother
warned him
never to cross streets
alone
he marched
around the corner
and marched
around the block

16

and marched
a long ways from home.

There
on a back street
of shimmery tar
that was wondrously
different
but frightfully far,

a pyramid sat
in the middle
of the street,
and there were sphinxes
and a zebra
and a tree
of singing parakeets.

And folks
in white body suits
tight and lean
bounced
and did tricks
on a great trampoline.

ow delighted Sudan was
to discover
their wild root hair,
how it fanned
like spokes of a wheel
in the afternoon breeze;
how it laughed
and hung down their backs
with a royal ease.

And he caught their eye
as he walked by;
he made them stop their
bouncing
to stare
at the giggling wings
the laid-back lagoons
and the mysterious lions
of his beautiful hair.

H|ey, sugah!" a familiar voice said
as a tall woman tumbled
over his head.
"Miss Pearl!" Sudan shouted, surprised
to see her again,
for he had always liked
his mother's tall friend.

"I'm traveling with the circus now,"
Pearl Poet said.
"This is my family. There's six of us.
We're known as THE FLYING DREADS."
"Say, youngblood," said a deep-voiced man,
"Come join us
for a while. Let's see what you can do
up here. Let's see your style."

So just to show off,
which he liked to do,
Sudan bopped to the trampoline
cool as could be
and hopped up
and bounced about,
and between you and me

it made him nervous
to bounce so high

but he loved to giggle
jump
tumble
and fly.

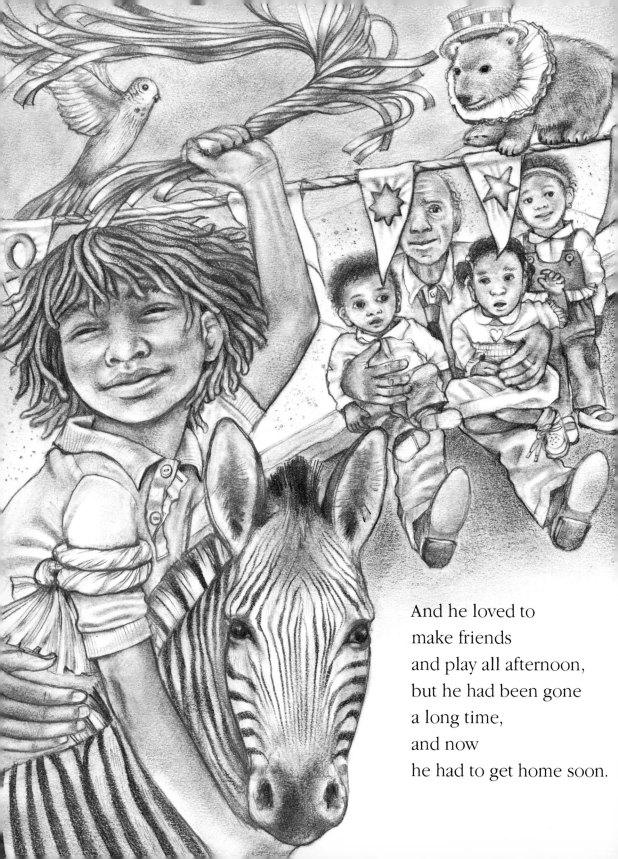

And he loved to
make friends
and play all afternoon,
but he had been gone
a long time,
and now
he had to get home soon.

 'll walk you home,"
said his mother's cheery friend.
"It'll be good to see the old block again."

Then she took his hand,
and street
after street
they walked, and they talked
about flying in the air
and how some people
act ugly
when they see
enchanted hair.

J ust be your pretty self, Sudan," she said
as they stopped at a corner
when the light changed
to red.
"And remember this, 'cause it's certainly true: Sticks
and stones might hurt your bones, but ugly words
shall never harm you."

And soon they came
to the door of his house,
where his mother waited
very upset,
but she hugged him
and kissed him,
then she scolded him too
for crossing all of those
big streets
by himself and do.

And she thanked
Pearl Poet
as they waved good-bye
and watched her
somersault
right before their eye
in a tumble of hair
as mysterious as sky.

nd up the house steps
Sudan followed his mother
and hopped and jumped around,
so excited was he
by the friends he had found.

And promising
never ever again
to wander away from home,
he eased into the bathroom
to be alone
in the mirror and stare
at the lions and locks,
at the wings
of his enchanted hair.

**W**hich he liked.

And that night
while his mother practiced
trumpet
before Sudan went to bed,
he sang to himself
a song of the words
Pearl Poet
left in his head.